Princess Peepers

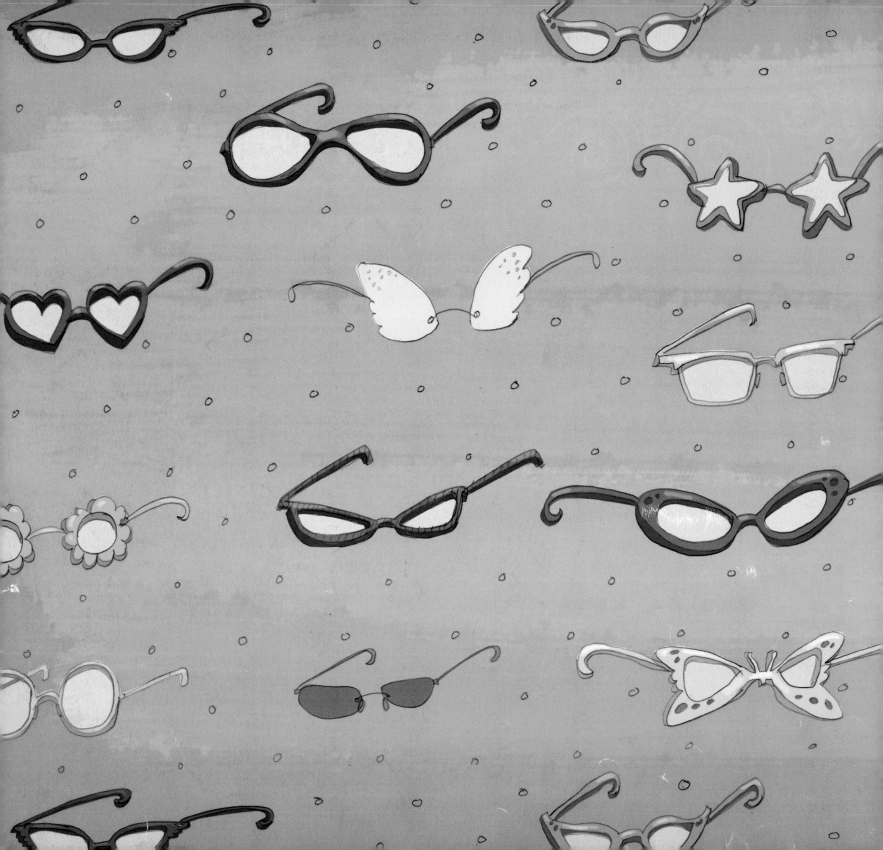

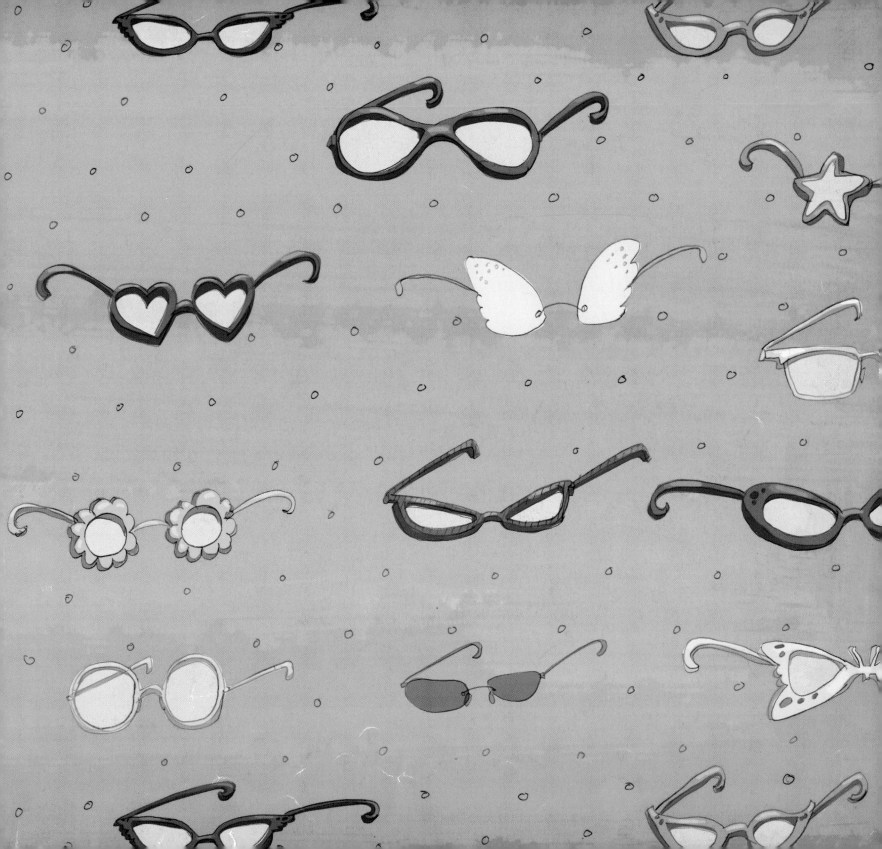

Princess Peepers

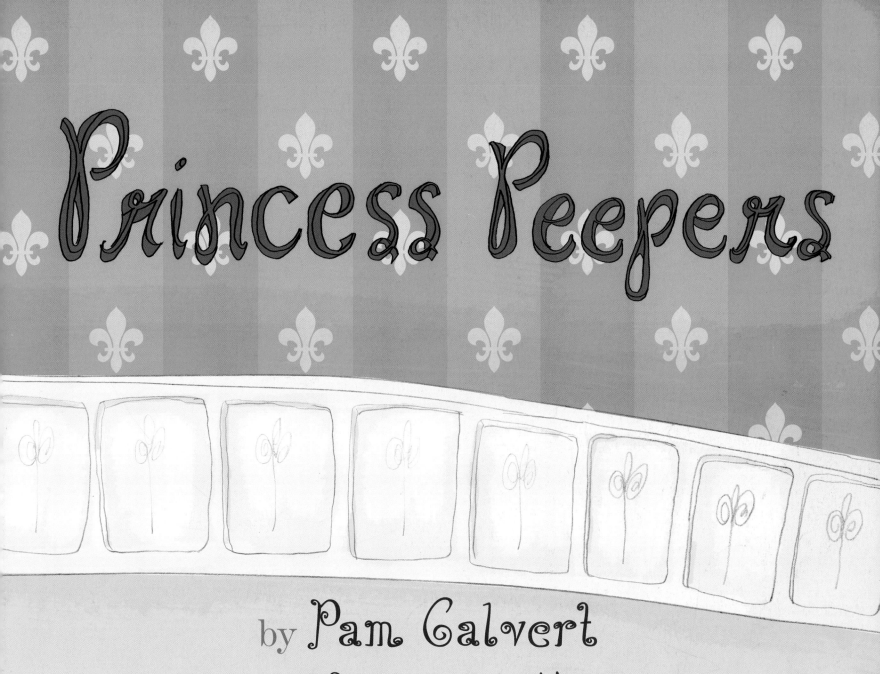

by Pam Calvert

illustrated by Tuesday Mourning

Marshall Cavendish Children

Text copyright © 2008 by Pam Calvert
Illustrations copyright © 2008 by Tuesday Mourning
First Marshall Cavendish paperback edition, 2011

Marshall Cavendish Corporation, 99 White Plains Road, Tarrytown, NY 10591
www.marshallcavendish.us/kids

Library of Congress Cataloging-in-Publication Data
Calvert, Pam
Princess Peepers / by Pam Calvert ; illustrated by Tuesday Mourning.—1st ed.
p. cm.
Summary: When the other princesses make fun of her for wearing glasses,
Princess Peepers vows to do without them, but after several mishaps—one
of which is especially coincidental—she admits that she really does need them if she wants to see.
978-0-7614-5437-3 (hardcover) 978-0-7614-5989-7 (paperback)
[1. Eyeglasses—Fiction. 2. Princesses—Fiction. 3. Humorous stories.] I. Mourning, Tuesday, ill. II. Title.
PZ7.C138Pr 2008   [E]dc22   2007022134

The illustrations are rendered in mixed media: graphite and digital/collage.

Book design by Anahid Hamparian
Editor: Marilyn Brigham
Printed in Malaysia (T)
1 3 5 6 4 2

To my helper and my parents,
who lovingly put up with me
not wearing my glasses
—P.C.

To Jon and Atticus—
thanks for all your
love and support
—T.M.

Princess Peepers loved to wear glasses.

In fact, she had different glasses for every occasion.

One of her favorites were the bug glasses she wore for her annual bug hunt.

She also liked the sparkly ones that went with her Halloween costume.

And her very favorites were her rose-colored glasses that matched her rose-colored roller skates.

But that all changed when she attended
The Royal Academy for Perfect Princesses.
"Oh, *m-my!*" one princess sputtered as
Princess Peepers entered the room. "What are
those on top of her nose?"

Another princess laughed. "It's an extra set of eyeballs, Grumbelina."

"You're wrong," said another. "She's an owl, not a princess."

Giggles and snorts filled the room.

The Royal Ball

Just then the Grand Matron bustled into the classroom. "Princesses, the Royal Ball will take place tonight. You will meet the Grand Prince!"

Princess Grumbelina whispered loudly, "Peepers better not show up with those horrible spectacles or she'll *be* a horrible spectacle."

The princesses snickered.

Princess Peepers raced out of the classroom.

Peepers ordered a footman to bring her trunk. She dumped in all of her glasses, including the ones on her nose.

"There." She sniffed. "Now I won't be different from the other princesses."

Satisfied, Princess Peepers flounced back to the classroom. She wanted to show Grumbelina and the others that she didn't need glasses. But no one was there.

"They are in the gardens, I believe," said a lady-in-waiting.

Princess Peepers skipped out of the school toward the royal greenhouse.

"There's Grumbelina," Peepers said as she ran over to the princess. "See? I don't need glasses."

"Neigh!" Grumbelina whinnied.

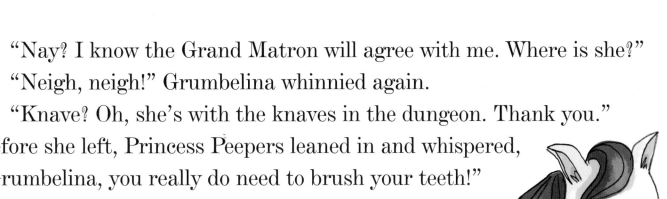

"Nay? I know the Grand Matron will agree with me. Where is she?"

"Neigh, neigh!" Grumbelina whinnied again.

"Knave? Oh, she's with the knaves in the dungeon. Thank you."

Before she left, Princess Peepers leaned in and whispered,

"Grumbelina, you really do need to brush your teeth!"

Peepers trotted off to the dungeon. There was quite a hubbub with guards going hither and thither.

"It sure smells good in this dungeon," Peepers said.

Then Peepers saw the Grand Matron lying on the floor! She was wearing her usual brown and white cloak. "Oh, Grand Matron! What have the knaves done to you?"

"Woof!" the Grand Matron barked.

"Roof? They threw you from the roof?" Peepers asked. "The scoundrels! I'll call the guards at once."

The princess turned
quickly and bumped into a
guard. The guard spilled
gooey mud and string all
over her.

"Holy pumpkins!
Watch yourself, guard," Peepers
ordered, "or you'll spill all over the
Grand Matron."

"I am very sorry, your highness," the guard said. "But I am not a guard. I am the chef! And that is not the Grand Matron. It is Duke, the royal mascot!"

"Jeepers!" Peepers cried. But then the princess remembered the ball. "I can't see the prince like this!" She dashed to her room to get ready.

The princess spent hours dressing herself so she'd look just right for the prince. "See?" Princess Peepers said to herself. "I don't need glasses."

When a lady-in-waiting came to check on the princess, Peepers asked, "How do I look?"

"Um . . . you look, um . . . remarkable!" the lady-in-waiting said.

The princess hurried toward the ballroom.

"Oh, fairydust!" the princess said. "I'm early." But this didn't fluster Princess Peepers. "I'll work on my dance steps while I'm waiting."

So she whirled and twirled around the room the way she would dance with the prince that night.

But she whirred and
whizzed and bobbled and
blurred right out the . . .

. . . WINDOW!

"Ahhhh!" Peepers screamed.

Fwump!
"Holy glass-slippers!" Peepers cried. "I'm so glad this horse was here." She patted the horse on the head.

"Madam," the horse said, "I am Prince Peerless last I checked."

"The Prince?" she cried. "Oh, magic-mirrors, I DO need my glasses!"

"You wear glasses?" the prince said. "Why, so do I."

It was love at first sight . . .

. . . after they put on their glasses!

And they all lived happily ever after.